BLUE BLOOD

MORE WILDSIDE CLASSICS

BLUE BLOOD

ARTHUR GRIFFITHS

WILDSIDE PRESS

BLUE BLOOD

This edition published 2005 by Wildside Press, LLC.
www.wildsidepress.com

BLUE BLOOD

CHAPTER I.

"The idea is simply preposterous. I decline to entertain it. I cannot listen to it—not for one moment. Never!"

The speaker was Mrs. Purling, "heiress of the Purlings"; imperious, emphatic, self-opinionated, as women become who have had their own way all their lives through.

"But, mother," went on Harold, her only son—like herself, large and broadly built; but, unlike her, quiet and rather submissive in manner, as one who had been habitually kept under — "I am really in earnest. I am absolutely sick of doing nothing."

"Because you won't do what you might. There is plenty for you to do. Has not the Duchess asked you to Scotland? You refuse — and such a splendid invitation! I have offered you a yacht. I say you may share a river in Norway with dear Lord Faro. I implore you to drive a coach, to keep racehorses, to take your place in the best society, as the representative of the Purling —"

"Pills?" put in Harold, with a queer smile.

His mother's face grew black instantly.

"Harold, do not dare to speak in that way. My father's memory should be respected by my only son."

Old Purling had made all his money by a certain chemical compound which had been adopted by the world at large as a panacea for every ill. But the heiress of the Purlings hated any reference to the Primeval Pills, although she owed to them her wealth.

"I want a profession," Harold said, returning to his point. "I want regular employment."

"Well, I say go into the Guards."

"I am too old. Besides, peace-soldiering, and in London, would never suit me, I know."

"Read law; it is a gentlemanly occupation."

"But most uninteresting. Now medicine —"

"Do not let me hear the word; the mere idea is intolerable. My son, the heir of the Purlings must not condescend so low."

"Considering my own father was a doctor," cried Harold, rather hotly.

"Not a mere doctor. A man of science, of world-wide repute, is not like a general practitioner, with a red lamp and an apothecary's shop, where he makes up —"

"Pills?" said Harold, again. He was throwing down the gauntlet indeed. Mrs. Purling had never known him like this before.

"Leave the room, Harold. I decline to speak to you further, or again, unless you appear in a more obedient and decorous frame of mind."

That Mrs. Purling was what she was, the chances of her life and her father were principally to blame. He had begun life as an errand-boy, and ended it as a millionnaire; but long before he ended he had forgotten the beginning. He had a sort of notion that he belonged to one of the old families in the county wherein he had bought wide estates, and he himself styled his only daughter "the heiress of the Purlings," as if there had been Purlings back for generations, and he was the last, not the first, of his race. It was he who had indoctrinated her with ideas of her own importance; and these same views had taken so strong a hold of him that he found it quite impossible to mate his daughter according to his mind. He was ambitious, as was natural to a *nouveau riche*; wide awake, or he would not have made so much money. Not one of the crowds of suitors who came forward was exactly to his taste. He would have preferred a man of title, but the peers who were not penniless were too proud; and the best baronet was an aged bankrupt, who had been twice through the courts, and enjoyed an indifferent name. It was strange that Isabel did not cut the Gordian knot, and choose for herself; but she was a duti-ful daughter, and little less cautious than her father. In the midst of it all he was called away on some particular business of his own — to another world — and Isabel was left alone, past thirty, and unmarried still.

The *rôle* of single blessedness may be charm-ing to a man of means, but it is often extremely irksome to an heiress in her own right. Miss Purling was like a pigeon that escapes from the inclosure at a match — an aim for every gun around. Great ladies took her up, as a kindness to their younger sons; briefless barristers, with visions of the Woolsack, besought her to help them to the first step — a seat in the House; clergymen with great views prayed her to join them in some stupendous charitable work, that must win for them the lawn-sleeves; more than one impecunious soldier pleaded with her for their tailors, whose bills without her help they were quite unable to pay. She seemed a common prey, fair game for every hand. This developed in her an undue amount of suspicion and a certain hardness of heart. She began to doubt whether there was one disinterested man in the whole world.

But before many years had passed she realised that unless she married there could be no prospect of peace. Already she had quarrelled with a dozen companions of her own sex; she wished now to try one of the other. But men seemed tired of proposing to her. She had the character of being as hard and cold as iron; and no one cared to run his head against a wall. If she wanted a husband now the proposal must come from her. Miss Purling in her heart rather liked the notion; it gave her a chance of posing like a queen in search of a consort, and years of independence had made her very queenlike and despotic indeed. So much so, that the only man to suit her must be a mere cipher without a will of his own; and he was difficult to find. Men of the kind are not plentiful unless they plainly perceive substantial advantage from assuming the part. But few guessed what kind of man would exactly suit Isabel Purling, so there were few pretenders.

Among those who flocked to her *soirées* — she was fond of entertaining in spite of her disabilities as a single woman — was a meek little professor, who lodged in Camden Town, and who came afoot in roomy goloshes, which now and again, in a fit of abstraction, he carried upstairs and laid upon the tea-table or at his hostess's feet, as though the carpet was damp and he feared she might run the risk of catarrh. He was reputed to be extremely erudite, a ripe scholar, and of some fame in scientific research. But of all his discoveries — and he had made many under the microscope and in space — the most surprising was the discovery that a lady who owned a deer-park and many thousands a-year desired him to make her his wife. But he was an obliging little man, always ready to do a kind thing for anybody; and he obliged Miss Purling in the way she wished — after all, at some cost to himself. The marriage meant little less than self-effacement for him; he was to take his wife's name instead of giving her his; he was to forego his favourite pursuits, and from an independent man of science pass into a mere appendage to the Purling property — part and parcel of his wife's goods and chattels as much as the park-palings, or her last-purchased dinner-service of rare old "blue."

It was odd that Miss Purling's choice should have fallen where it did; for her tendencies were decidedly upward, and she would have dearly loved to be styled "my lady," and to have moved freely in the society of the "blue-blooded of the land." It was her distrustfulness which had stood in the way. She feared that in an aristocratic alliance she could not have made her own terms. And with the results of this marriage with Dr. Purling — as he was henceforth styled — she had every reason to be pleased. He proved a most exemplary husband — the chief of her subjects, nothing more; a loyal, unpretending vassal, who did not ask to share the purple, but was content to sit upon the steps of the throne. He continued a shy, reserved, unobtrusive little man to the end of the chapter; and the chapter was closed without unnecessary delay as soon as the birth of a son secured the succession of the Purling estates. Dr. Purling felt there was nothing more required of him, so he quietly died.

His widow raised a tremendous tablet to his memory, eulogising his scientific attainments and domestic worth; but, although she appeared inconsolable, she was secretly pleased to have the uncontrolled education of her infant son. An elderly lady with a baby-boy is like a girl with a doll — just as the little mother dresses and undresses its counterfeit presentment of a child in wax and rags, crooning over its tiny cradle, talking to it in baby-language, pretending to watch with anxious solicitude its every mood, so Mrs. Purling found in Harold a plaything of which she never tired. She coddled and cosseted him to her heart's content. If he had cried for the moon some effort would have been made to obtain for him the loan of that pale planet, or the best substitute for it that could be got for cash. If his finger ached, or he had a pain in his big toe, he was physicked with half the Pharmacopœia; he underwent divers systems of regimen, was kept out of draughts, cautioned against chills, cased in red flannel; he might, to crown all, have been laid by in cotton-wool. His mother's over-much care ought to have killed him; but he had inherited from her a fine physique, and the lad was large-limbed, healthy, and well grown.

And this vigilant supervision was prolonged far beyond the time when youths are emancipated usually from their mother's control. Long after he had left college, and was launched out upon the world, she kept her hands upon the reins, ruling him with a sharp bit, and driving him the road she decided it was best for him to go. Mrs. Purling had grown more and more imperious with advancing years, impatient of contradiction, self-satisfied, very positive that everything she did was right. She could not brook opposition to her wishes. Those who dared to thwart her must do it at their peril; no nature but one entirely subservient would be likely to continue permanently in accord with hers; and it was easy to predict troubles in the future between mother and son unless he yielded always a complete and docile submission to her will.

For a long time Harold wore his chains without a murmur. Obedient deference had been a habit with him from childhood, and, however irksome and galling the slavery, it was not until he had made practical acquaintance with the actual value of the life she wished him to lead that there arose in him a disposition to rebel. Mrs. Purling had all along been chafed with the notion that she did not enjoy that social distinction to which as a wealthy woman she considered herself entitled. In her own estimation she ranked very high; but the best families of the neighbourhood did not accept her valuation. Some went so far as to call her a vulgar old snob; and "snobbish," as we understand the word, she certainly was. She worshipped rank; and it was a very sore point with her that she was not freely admitted into the best society of the county in which she lived. She looked to Harold to redress her wrongs. Where she failed, a handsome young fellow, of engaging presence and heir to a fine estate, must assuredly succeed. He might, if he chose, be acceptable anywhere. There was no limit to her dreams. He might mate with a duke's daughter; and after such an alliance — who would presume to question the social rights of the Purlings?

It was therefore her chief and greatest desire to make a man of fashion of her son. Her purse was long — he might dip into it as deep as he pleased. Let him but take his proper position, on an equality with the noblest and best, and all charges would be gladly defrayed by her. She wanted him to be a dandy, *répandu* in society, a member of the Coaching Club, well known at Prince's, at Hurlingham, at Lord's; sought after by dowagers; intimate with royalties; she would not have seriously resented a reputation for a little wickedness, provided he erred in the right direction — with people of the blue blood, that is to say — and the scandal did not go too far.

Unhappily, Harold's tastes and inclinations lay all in the opposite direction. In external appearance he favoured his mother, in disposition he was his father's son. Like him reserved — he would have been shy but for his training at school and college, which had rubbed the sensitive skin off his self-consciousness; like him studious too, thoughtful, quiet, with scientific tastes and proclivities. His friends in familiar talk called him "Old Steady"; he had never got into debt or serious trouble. Even in the midst of the whirling maze of London life he continued steadfastly sober and sedate.

Here at once was to be found the germ of discord between mother and son, the first gap or chink in their friendly relations, which might widen some day into a yawning breach. But yet Mrs. Purling could find no fault with her son. She might resent the staid sober-mindedness of his conduct; but she was perforce compelled to confess that he was a dear good son, affectionate, devoted, considerate; and there was much solid comfort in the thought that the good name of the Purlings, as well as their substantial wealth, could be safely intrusted to his hands. This she readily allowed; and, had he continued obedient and tractable until he was grey-haired, Mrs. Purling might have gone down into her grave without a shadow of excuse for quarreling with her son.

It was when he was past five-and-twenty that there arose between them misunderstanding, at first only a small cloud no bigger than a man's hand. Harold suddenly declared that he was sick of gallivanting about the fashionable world; sick of idleness — sick of the silly purposeless existence he led; and thereupon announced his intention of studying medicine seriously and as a profession. Mrs. Purling was at first aghast, then argumentative, finally indignant. But Harold remained inflexible, and she grew more and more wrathful. It led at length to something like a rupture between them. She received the news of his success in the schools with grim contempt, condescending only to ask once whether he wished her to buy him a practice, or whether he meant to put up a red lamp at the family-mansion in Berkeley Square.

Her persistent implacability gave Harold much pain, but he did not despair of bringing her round in the end; only, to avoid further dissensions, he wisely resolved to keep out of her way: and as soon as he had gained his diploma he started for Germany, intending to prosecute his studies abroad.

CHAPTER II.

It was not until he had been absent more than a year that Mrs. Purling appeared to relent. She began to yearn after her son; she missed him and was disposed to be reconciled, provided he would but meet her halfway. At first she sent olive-branches in the shape of munificent letters of credit over and above his liberal allowance; then came more distinct overtures in lengthy epistles, which grew daily warmer in tone and plainly showed that her resentment was passing rapidly away. These letters of hers were her chief pleasure in life; she prided herself on her ability to wield the pen. When, instead of a few curt sentences in brief acknowledgment of his letters, his mother resumed her old custom of filling several sheets of post with advice, gossip, odds and ends of news, mixed with stray scraps of wisdom culled from Martin Tupper, Harold began to hope that the worst was over and that he would soon be forgiven in set form.

And he was right. Pardon was soon extended to him, not quite unconditional, but weighted merely with terms which — Mrs. Purling thought — no sensible man could hesitate to accept.

She only asked him to settle in life. He must

marry some day — why not soon? Not to any-body, of course — he must be on his guard against foreign intriguing sirens, who would en-tangle him if they could — but to some lady of rank and fashion, fitted by birth and breeding to be the mother of generations of Purlings yet to be. This was the condition she annexed to for-giveness of the past; this the text upon which she preached in her letters week after week. The doctrine of judicious marriage appeared in all she wrote with the unfailing regularity of the red thread that runs through all the strands of Ad-miralty rope.

Harold smiled at the reiteration of these sen-timents; smiled, but he had misgivings. Herein might be another source of disagreement be-tween his mother and himself. Would their re-spective opinions agree as to the style of girl most likely to suit him? Then he began to con-sider what style of girl his mother would choose; and while he was thus musing there came a mis-sive which plainly showed Mrs. Purling's hand.

"I have been at Compton Revel for a week —"

"I wonder," thought Harold, when he had read thus far, "why they asked her there? My dear old mother must have been in the seventh heaven of delight. She always longed to be on more intimate terms with Lady Calverly."

"I have been at Compton Revel for a week," his mother said, "and met there a Miss Fan-shawe, one of Lord Fanshawe's daughters, who seemed to me quite the nicest girl I have ever known. I took to her directly; and without conceit I may be permitted to say that I think she took quite as readily to me. We became immense friends. She was at such pains to be agreeable to an uninteresting old woman like myself that I feel convinced she has a good heart. I confess I was charmed with her. It is not only that she is strikingly handsome, but her whole bearing and her style are so distinguished that she might be descended from a long line of kings — as I make no doubt she is.

"Of course she has moved only in the best circles; her mother being dead, she has been introduced by the Countess of Gayfeather, and goes with her ladyship everywhere. Just imagine, she has been to State-balls at the Palace; the Prince has danced with her, and she has been spoken to by the Princess! You know how I enjoy hearing all the news of the great world, and Miss Fanshawe has been so obliging as to amuse me for hours with descriptions of all she has seen and heard — not a little, I assure you; she is not one of those flighty girls who have no ears but for flattery, no eyes but for young men; she is observant, critical perhaps, but strikingly just in her strictures on what goes on around. I find she has thought out several of the complex problems of our modern high-pressure life; and really she gave me very valuable ideas upon my favourite theory of 'lady-helps,' to which I am devoting now so much of my spare time.

"Miss Fanshawe has promised to pay me a long visit at Purlington some day soon — a real act of kindness which I fully appreciate. It will indeed be a treat to a lonely old woman to find so entertaining a guest and companion.

"When do you think of returning? Gollop tells me there are plenty of pheasants this year. Surely, you have had enough of those dry German *savants* and that dull university-town?"

The hook was rather coarsely baited; it would hardly have deceived the most guileless and unsuspecting. Harold Purling at a glance could read between the lines; he could trace effect to cause, and readily understood why his mother was so anxious for his return.

"One of Lady Gayfeather's girls, is she? I never thought much of that lot. However — but why on earth should Lady Calverly take my dear mother up in this way, at the eleventh hour?"

He would have wondered yet more if he had seen how cordially Mrs. Purling had been welcomed to Compton Revel.

"It is so good of you to come to us," Lady Calverly said, with effusion. "We are so glad to have you here, and have looked forward to it for so long."

For about seventeen years, in fact, during which time Lord and Lady Calverly had completely ignored the existence of their near neighbour, Mrs. Purling. Compton Revel might have been a paradise, and the heiress an exiled peri waiting at the gates.

The party assembled was after Mrs. Purling's own heart. They were all great people, at least in name; and the heiress of the Purlings was heard to murmur that she did like to be in such good society — she felt so perfectly at home. And they all made much of her. One night she was handed in to dinner by a Duke, another by an ex-Cabinet Minister. The latter made her feel proud, for the first time in her life, of her son, and the line he had adopted so sorely against her will.

"Mr. Purling's paper on toxicology," he said, "is quite the cleverest thing that has appeared on the subject. My friend, Sir William —" he mentioned a physician of world-wide repute — "considers that Mr. Purling will go far."

Lady Calverly followed suit by declaring that Mr. Purling was a pattern young man, everyone gave him so good a character. They *did* hope to see him at Compton Revel directly he got back to England.

Then Miss Fanshawe metaphorically prostrated herself before Mrs. Purling, and by judicious phrases and ready sympathy completely won her good-will.

"You certainly made an impression upon her, Phillipa," said Lady Calverly afterwards.

"She is a vain and rather silly old woman," Miss Fanshawe replied. Language that might have opened Mrs. Purling's eyes.

"But I am very glad you became such good friends. Purlington is a very desirable place."

Here, then, was a faint clue to the mystery of Mrs. Purling's tardy reception at Compton Revel. Intrigue — not necessarily base, but covered by the harmless phrase, "It would be so very nice" — was at work to bring about a match between Miss Fanshawe and Harold Purling. She was one of a large family of girls and her father was an impoverished peer. Besides, her career so far had not been an unmixed success. Lady Gayfeather's young ladies had the reputation of being the "quickest" in the town.

"I have met the son," went on Lady Calverly.

"Yes?" Phillipa's tone was one of absolute indifference.

"He is a gentleman."

"I have always heard of him as a solemn prig — 'Old Steady' he was named at college. I confess I have no special leaning to these very proper and decorous youths."

"Do not say that you are harping still on that old affair. I assure you Gilly Jillingham is unworthy of you. You are not thinking still of each other, I sincerely hope?"

"I may be of him," said Phillipa bitterly. "He is not likely to think of any one — but himself."

"I shall never forgive myself for surrendering you to Lady Gayfeather. Nothing but misery seems to hang about her and her house. This last affair —"

There had been a terrible scandal, not many months old, and hardly forgotten yet, which had roused Lady Calverly to remove her cousin, Phillipa Fanshawe, from the evil influences of Lady Gayfeather's set. Whether or not the rescue had come in time it would be difficult to say. Miss Fanshawe could hardly escape scot-free from her associations, nor was it to her advantage that rumour had bracketed her name with that of a successful but not popular man of fashion. There had been a talk of marriage, but he had next to nothing; no more had she.

"We must have an end to all that," said Lady Calverly decisively. "You must promise me to forget Mr. Jillingham for good and all."

"Of course," replied Phillipa; but the pale face and that sad look in her weary eyes belied her words.

It seemed as if she had shot her bolt at the target of life's happiness, and that the arrow had fallen very wide of the gold.

CHAPTER III.

When old Purling bought the — shire estates there was an ancient manor-house on the property, a picturesque but inconvenient residence, which did not at all come up to his ideas of a country gentleman's place. It was therefore incontinently pulled down, and one of the most fashionable architects of the day, having *carte blanche* to build, erected a Palladian pile of wide frontage and imposing dimensions on the most prominent site he could find. It ought to have haunted its author like a crime; but he was spared, and the punishment fell upon the innocent who dwelt around. There was no escape from Purlington, so long as you were within a dozen miles of it. Wherever you went and wherever you looked, down from points of vantage or up from quiet dells, this great white caravanserai, with its glittering plate-glass panes and staring stucco, forced itself upon you with the unblushing effrontery of a brazen beauty, with painted face and bedizened in flaunting attire. But the heiress thought it was a very splendid place, with its pineries, conservatories, its acres of glass, and its army of retainers in liveries of rainbow hues. Mrs. Purling was a little afraid of her servants, albeit strong-minded in other respects; but it was natural she should submit to a coachman who had once worn the royal livery, or quail before a butler who had lived with a duke.

The butler met Harold on his return, extending to him a gracious patronising welcome, as if he were doing the honours of his own house.

"Misterarold," he cried, making one word of the name and title, "this is a pleasant surprise. You wus not expected, sir; not in the least."

"My mother is at home?"

"No, sir; out. In the kerridge. She drove Homersham way."

"See after my things. Here are my keys." And Harold passed on to the little morning-room which Mrs. Purling called her own. Having the choice of half a dozen chambers, each as big as Exeter Hall, she preferred to occupy habitually the smallest den in the house. To his surprise he found the room not untenanted. A young lady was at the book-case, and she turned seemingly in trepidation on hearing the door open.

"Miss Fanshawe," thought Harold, as he advanced with eyes that were unmistakably critical.

"I must introduce myself," he said. "I am Harold."

"The last of the Saxon kings?"

"No; the first of the Purling princes. I know you quite well. Has my mother never mentioned me?"

"I only arrived yesterday," the young lady replied, rather evading the question.

"My mother must be delighted. She told me she was looking forward eagerly to your promised visit."

"She really spoke of me?"

"In her letters; again and again."

"I hardly thought —"

"That you had taken her by storm? You have; and I was surprised, for she is not easily won."

Not a civil speech, which this girl only resented by placing a pair of old-fashioned double glasses across her small nose, and looking at him with a gravity that was quite comical.

"But now that I have met you I can readily understand."

The same look through the glasses; sphinx-like, she seemed impervious both to depreciation and compliment.

"And she has left you alone all the morning? I am afraid you must have been bored."

"Thank you. I had my work."

It was an exquisite piece of art needlework. Water-lilies and yellow irises on a purple ground. She confessed it was her own design.

"And books?"

He took up Schlegel's *Philosophy of History* in the original.

"You read German?"

"O yes."

"And Italian? and French? and Sanscrit — without doubt?"

"Not quite; but I have looked into Max Müller, and know something of Monier Williams."

And this was one of Lady Gayfeather's girls! Was this a new process, the last dodge in the perpetual warfare between maidens and mankind?

Harold looked at the prodigy.

In appearance she was quite unlike the conventional type of a London young lady of fashion. Her fresh dimpled cheeks wore roses and a pearly bloom that spoke of healthy hours and a tranquil life; her dress was quiet almost to plainness; there was nothing modern in the style of her coiffure; Lobb would not have been proud of her boots. Her fair white hands were innocent of rings; she wore no jewelry; there was no gold or silver about her, except for the gold-rimmed glasses that made so curious a contrast to her young face, with its merry eyes and frame of mutinous curls.

"You will not be angry," said Harold earnestly, "if I tell you that you are not in the least what I expected to find you, Miss Fanshawe —"

"Miss Fanshawe!" Her gay laugh was infectious. "I'm afraid —"

But just now the butler came in to say that the carriage was coming up the drive. Harold went out to meet his mother, without noticing that the young lady also got up and hurriedly left the room.

"It's just like you, you stupid boy!" said the heiress. "Why did you give me no notice?"

"I meant to have written from Paris. But it's all for the best. You were quite right. She is perfectly charming."

"Who?"

"Miss Fanshawe. I have made her acquaintance."

"In town?"

"No, here; in your own morning-room."

"What!" The ejaculation contained volumes. "Was there ever anything so annoying! But it is all your fault for coming so unexpectedly."

"What harm? We introduced ourselves, Miss Fanshawe —"

"Miss Fiddlesticks! That's Dolly Driver, your father's cousin!"

"Indeed! Then I wish I had made the acquaintance of my father's cousins a little earlier in life. Why have I been kept in ignorance of my relatives? Where do they live?"

Mrs. Purling, instead of answering him, took him by the arm abruptly, as if to ask him some searching question; then suddenly checking herself, she said —

"Have you had lunch? It must be ready. Come into the dining-room."

"Will not Miss Driver join us?"

"She will go to the housekeeper's room, where she ought to have been sitting, and not in my boudoir."

"Mother!"

"It's as well to be plain-spoken. Dolly Driver is not of our rank in life. Her parents are miserably poor. Nevertheless," — as if the crime hardly deserved such liberal pardon — "I am not indisposed to help them. She is going to a situation."

"Poor girl! Companion or governess? or both?"

"Neither; she will be either housemaid or undernurse."

Harold almost jumped off his chair.

"A girl like that! as a domestic servant! Mother, it's a disgraceful shame!"

"The disgrace is in the language you permit yourself to use to me. Your travels have made you rather boisterous and *gauche*. What disgrace can there be in honest work? Household work is honourable, and was once occupation for the daughters of kings. Happily the world grows more sensible. I look to the day as not far distant when the wide-spread employment of lady-helps will solve that terrible problem — the redundancy of girls."

"My cousin will not continue redundant, I feel sure."

"She is not your cousin."

"Whether or no, she should be spared the

degradation you propose. She is a girl of culture, highly educated. You cannot condemn her to the kitchen."

"The lady-helps have their own apartment; but I decline to justify myself."

And Mrs. Purling lapsed into silence. There was friction between them already.

"Where are you going?" she asked, when lunch was over.

"To the housekeeper's room."

"Harold, I forbid you. It's highly improper — it's absolutely indelicate."

"She is my cousin; besides there is a *chaperone*, Mrs. Haigh, or I'll call in the cook."

"Do you mean to set me at defiance?"

"I mean to do what I consider right, even although my views may not coincide with yours, mother."

For the rest of the day, indeed, Harold never left his newly-found cousin's side. The heiress fumed and fretted, and scolded, but all in vain. There was a new kind of masterfulness about her son which for the moment she was powerless to resist.

"Of course she will dine with us," Harold said. And of course she did, although Mrs. Purling looked as if she wished every mouthful would choke her. Of course Harold called her Dolly to her face; was she not his cousin? Quite as naturally he would have given her a cousinly kiss when he said good-night, but something in her pure eyes and modest face restrained him.

Certainly she was the nicest girl he had ever met in his life.

"Where's Doll?" he asked next morning at breakfast. "Not down?"

"Miss Driver is halfway to London, I hope," replied Mrs. Purling, curtly. She was not a bad general, and had taken prompt measures already to recover from her temporary reverse.

"I shall go after her."

"If you do, you need not trouble to return."

Nothing more was said, but anger filled the hearts of both mother and son.

CHAPTER IV.

"I expect my dear friend, Miss Fanshawe, in a few days, Harold. I trust you will treat her becomingly."

"One would think I was a bear just escaped from the Zoo. Why should you fear discourtesy from me to any lady?"

"Because she is a friend of mine. Of late you seemed disposed to run counter to me in every respect."

"I have no such desire, I assure you," said Harold, gravely; and there the matter ended.

The preparation for Miss Fanshawe's reception could not have been more ambitious if she had been a royal princess. With much reluctance Mrs. Purling eschewed triumphal arches and a brass band, but she redecorated the best bedroom, and sent two carriages to the station, although her guest could hardly be expected to travel in both.

"*This* is Miss Fanshawe," said the heiress, with much emphasis — "the Honourable Miss Fanshawe."

"The Honourable Miss Fanshawe is only a very humble personage, not at all deserving high-sounding titles," said the young lady for herself. "My name is Phillipa — to my friends, and as such I count you, dear Mrs. Purling; perhaps some day I may be allowed to say the same of your son."

She spoke rapidly, with the fluent ease natural to a well-bred woman. In the subdued light of the cosy room Harold made out a tall, slight figure, well set off by the tight-fitting ulster; she carried her head proudly, and seemed aristocratic to her finger-tips.

"I should have known you anywhere, Mr. Purling," she went on, without a pause. "You are so like your dear mother. You have the same eyes."

It was a wonder she did not use the adjective "sweet"; for her tone clearly implied that she admired them.

"I hear you are desperately and astoundingly clever," she continued, like the brook flowing on for ever. "They tell me your pamphlet on vivisection was quite masterly. How proud you must be, Mrs. Purling, to hear such civil things said of his books!"

"Do you take sugar?" Harold asked, as he put a cup of tea into a hand exquisitely gloved.

She looked up at him sharply, but failed to detect any satire behind his words.

Harold thought that there was too much sugar and butter about her altogether. Even thus early he felt antipathetic; yet, when they were seated at dinner, and had an opportunity of observing her at leisure, he could not deny that she was handsome, in a striking, queenly sort of way; but he thought her complexion was too pale, and, at times, when off her guard, a worn-out, harassed look came over her face, and a tinge of melancholy clouded her dark eyes. But it was not easy to find her off her guard. The unceasing strife of several seasons had taught her to keep all the world at sword-point; she was armed *cap-à-pie*, and ready always to fight with a clever woman's keenest weapons — her eyes and tongue. Upon Harold she used both with consummate skill; it was clear that she wished to please him, addressing herself principally to him, asking his opinion on scientific questions, coached up on purpose, and listening attentively when he replied.

"How wise you have been to keep away from town these years! One gets so sick of the perpetual round."

"I should have thought it truly delightful," said Mrs. Purling, who, of course, took the unknown for the magnificent.

"Any honest labour would be preferable."

"Turn lady-help; that's my mother's common advice."

"Harold, how dare you suggest such a thing to Miss Fanshawe? Do you know she is a peer's daughter?"

"I thought you said housework would do for the daughters of kings; and you have proposed it to our cousin, Dolly Dri —"

"Were you at Ryde this year, Phillipa?" asked Mrs. Purling, promptly.

"No — at Cowes. We were yachting. Dreary business, don't you think, Mr. Purling?"

"I rather like it."

"Yes, if you have a pleasant party and an object. But mere cruising" — Miss Fanshawe was quick at shifting her ground.

"And you are going to Scotland?"

"Probably; and then for a round of visits. Dear, dear, how I loathe it all! I had far rather stay with you."

The heiress smiled gratefully. It was, indeed, the dearest wish of her heart that Phillipa should stay with her for good and all, and she was at no pains to conceal the fact. To Phillipa she spoke with diffidence, doubting whether this great personage could condescend to favour her son. But there was no lack of frankness in the old lady's speech.

"If you and he would only make a match of it!"

Miss Fanshawe squeezed Mrs. Purling's hand affectionately.

"I like him, I confess. More's the pity. I'm sure he detests me."

"As if it were possible!"

"Trust a girl to find out whether she's appreciated. Mr. Purling, for my sins, positively dislikes me; or else he has seen some one already to whom he has given his heart."

Mrs. Purling shook her head sadly, remembering artful Dolly Driver.

"You do not know all your son's secrets; no mother does."

"I do know this one, I fear."

And then Mrs. Purling described the absurd mistake in identity.

"You are not angry?" she went on. "For my part, I was furious. But nothing shall come of it, I solemnly declare. Harold will hardly risk my serious displeasure; but he shall know that, sooner than accept this creature as my daughter, I would banish him for ever from my sight."

"It will not come to that, I trust," said Phillipa, earnestly, and with every appearance of good faith.

"Not if you will help me, as I know you will."

Mrs. Purling was resolved now to issue positive orders for Harold to marry Miss Fanshawe — out of hand. But next day Phillipa suddenly announced her intention of returning to town.

"You promised to stay at least a month." The heiress was in tears.

"I am heartily sorry; but Cæcilia — Lady Gayfeather — is ill and alone. I must go to her at once."

"You have a feeling heart, Phillipa. This is a sacred duty; I cannot object. But I shall see you again?"

"As soon as I can return, dear Mrs. Purling — if you will have me, that is to say."

The story of Lady Gayfeather's illness was a mere fabrication. What summoned Phillipa to London was this note:

"I *must* see you. Can you be at Cæcilia's on Saturday? — G."

Phillipa sat alone in Lady Gayfeather's drawing-room, when Mr. Jillingham was announced.

"What does this mean?" she asked.

"I'm broke, simply."

"You don't look much like it."

To say the truth, he did not; he never did. He had had his ups and downs; but if he was down he hid away in outer darkness; if you saw him at all, he was floating like a jaunty cork on the very top of the wave. He was a marvel to everyone; it was a mystery how he lasted so long. Money went away from him as rain runs off the oiled surface of a shiny mackintosh coat. And yet he had always plenty of it; eclipses he might know, but they were partial; collapse might threaten, but it was always delayed. He had still the best dinners, the best cigars, the best brougham; was *bien vu* in the best society: had the best boot-varnish in London, and wore the most curly-brimmed hats, the envy of every hatter but his own. To all outward seeming there was no more fortunate prosperous man about town; the hard shifts to which he had been put at times were known only to himself — and to one other man, who had caught him tripping once, and found his account in the fact. The pressure this man excited drove Gilly Jillingham nearly to despair. He was really on the brink of ruin at this moment, although he stood before Phillipa as reckless and defiant as when he had first won her girlish affections, and thrown them carelessly on one side.

"How can I help you?" asked Phillipa, when he had repeated his news.

"I never imagined you could; but you take such an interest in me, I thought you might like to know."

"And you have dragged me up to London simply to tell me this?"

"Certainly. You always took a delight in coming when I called."

It was evident that he had a strong hold over her. She trembled violently.

"Are these lies I hear?" he went on, speaking with mocking emphasis. "Can it be possible you mean to marry that cub?"

"Who has been telling you this?"

"Answer my question."

"What right have you to ask?"

"The best. You know it. Have you not been promised to me since — since —"

"Well, do you wish me to redeem my promise? I am ready to marry you now — today, if you please. Ruined as you are, reckless, unprincipled, gambler — I know not what —"

"That's as well. But I am obliged to you; I will not trespass on your good-nature. I shall have enough to do to keep myself."

"We might go to a colony."

"I can fancy you in the bush!"

"Anything would be preferable to the false, hollow life I lead. I want rest. I could pray for it. I long to lay my head peacefully where —"

"Wherever you please. Try Mr. Purling's shoulder. You have my full permission."

Phillipa's eyes flashed fire at this heartless *persiflage*.

"There is no such luck."

"Can he dare to be indifferent? How you must hate him!"

"As I did you."

"And do still? Thank you. But I wish you joy. When is it to be?"

"I tell you there is absolutely nothing between us. Mr. Purling is, to the best of my belief, engaged already."

"Not with his mother's consent, surely? Why, then, has she made so much of you?"

"No; not with her consent; indeed, it is quite against her wish. Mrs. Purling as much as told me that if her son married this cousin he would be disinherited. They do not agree very well together now."

"It's all hers — the old woman's — in her

own right?"

"So far as I know."

Gilly Jillingham lay back in his chair and mused for a while.

"It's not a bad game if the cards play true."

His evil genius, had he been present, might have hinted that sometimes the cards played for Mr. Jillingham a little too true.

"Not a bad game. Phillipa, how do you stand with this old beldame?"

"She pretends the most ardent affection for me."

"There are no other relatives, no one she would take up if this son gave unpardonable offence?"

"Not that I know of. Besides, she calls me her dear daughter already."

"And would adopt you, doubtless, if the cub were got out of the way. Yes, it can be done, I believe, and you can do it, Phillipa, if you please. Only persuade the old lady to make you the heiress of the Purlings, and there will be an end to your troubles — and mine."

Soon after this conversation Miss Fanshawe returned to Purlington. The heiress smothered her with caresses.

"I shall not let you go away again. We have missed you more than I can say."

"And you also, Mr. Harold? Are you glad to see me again?"

Harold bowed courteously.

"Of course; I have been counting the hours to Miss Fanshawe's return."

"Fibs! I can't believe it."

By-and-by she came to him.

"Why cannot we be friends, Mr. Purling? It pains me to be hated as you hate me."

"You are really quite mistaken," Harold began.

"I am ready to prove my friendship. I know all about Miss Driver — there!"

"Do you know where she is at this present moment?" Harold asked, eagerly.

"You really wish to know? Your mother will tell me, I daresay. How hard hit you must be! But there is my hand on it. You shall have all the help that I can give."

Next day she told him.

"Miss Driver is at Harbridge."

"In service?"

"No; at home. They live there. Her father is a Custom-house officer."

That evening Harold informed his mother that important business called him away. She remonstrated. How could he leave the house while Miss Fanshawe was still there? What was the business? At least he might tell his mother; or it might wait. She could not allow him to leave.

Mere waste of words; Harold was off next morning to Harbridge, and Phillipa reported progress to her co-conspirator.

"It promises well," said Gilly. "I may be able to muzzle that scoundrel after all."

CHAPTER V.

A quaint old red-sandstone town; the river-harbour crowded with small craft, but now and again, like a Triton among the minnows, a timber-brig or a trading-barque driven in by stress of weather. When the tide went out — as it did seemingly with no intention of coming back, it went so far — the long level sands were spotted with groups of fisherfolk, who dug with pitchforks for sand-eels; while in among the rocks an army of children gleaned great harvests of a kind of seaweed, which served for food when times were hard.

These rocks were the seaward barrier and break-water of the little port, and did their duty well when, as now, they were tried by the full force of a westerly gale. It is blowing great guns; the hardy sheep that usually browse upon the upland slopes must starve perforce today — they cannot stand upon the steep incline; the cocks and hens of the cottagers take refuge to leeward of their homes; every gust is laden with atoms of sand or stone, which strike like hail or small shot upon the face. See how the waves dash in at the outlying rocks, hurrying onward like bloodhounds in full cry, scuffling, struggling, madly jostling one another in eagerness to be first in the fray; joining issue with tremendous crash, only to be spent, broken, dissipated into thin air. Overhead the sky changes almost with the speed of the blast; sometimes the sun winks from a corner of the leaden clouds and tinges with glorious light the foam-bladders as they burst and scatter around their clouds of spray; in between the headlands the sea is churned into creaming froth, as though the housewives of the sea-gods with unwearying arms were whipping "trifle" for some tremendous bridal-feast.

The houses at Harbridge mostly faced the shore, but all had stone porches, and the doors stood not in front, but at one side. The modest cottage which Mr. Driver called his own was like the rest; but as he enters, for all his care, a keen knife-edged gust of the pushing wind precedes him and announces his return. Next instant the little lobby is filled: a bevy of daughters, the good house-mother, one or two youngsters dragging at his legs, everyone eager to welcome the breadwinner home. They divest him of his wraps, soothing him the while with that tender loving solicitude a man finds only at his own happy hearth.

He unfolds his budget of news: a lugger driven by stress of weather upon the Castle Rock; suspicions of smuggling among the rough beyond Langness Cove; Dr. Holden's new partner arrived last night.

"I have asked him to come up this evening. A decent sort of chap."

Forthwith they fired a volley of questions. Was he old or young, married or single? had he blue eyes or brown? and how was he called?

To all papa makes shift to reply. The name he had forgotten, also the colour of his hair; but the fellow had eyes and two arms and two legs; he did not squint; had a pleasant address and all the appearance of an unmarried man.

"How could you see that, wise father?" asked Doll.

"He looked so sheepish when I mentioned my daughters. Doubtless he had heard of you, Miss Doll, and of your dangerous wiles."

She pinched his ear. They were excellent friends, were father and eldest daughter. Mr. Driver, a scholar and a man of letters, who had been thankful to exchange an uncertain footing upon the lower rungs of the ladder of literature for a small post under Government, had for years devoted his talents to the education of the children. In Dolly, as his most apt pupil, he took a peculiar pride.

"Come in, doctor!" cried Mr. Driver that night. "We are all dying, but only to make your acquaintance."

The new visitor was checked at the very threshold by Dolly's cry —

"Mr. Purling!"

And Harold stood confessed to his cousins

without a chance of further disguise.

"Cousin Harold, you mean," he said, as he offered Dolly his hand.

She tried hard to hide her blushes; and then and there Mrs. Driver, after the manner of mothers, built up a great castle in the air, which her husband shook instantly to its foundations by asking unceremoniously and not without a shade of angry suspicion in his tone —

"Why did you not claim relationship this morning?"

He disliked the notion of a man stealing into his house under false colours.

"I waited for you to speak. You heard my name."

"I did not catch it clearly. Besides, I had never heard of you. None of us have. Your mother did not choose to recognise the relationship."

"She called you a tide-waiter," said his wife indignantly.

"At least I'm not a white-tied waiter," cried Mr. Driver, with a laugh, in which all joined. Then in low voice Dolly said —

"I met Mr. Purling at Purlington."

At which her father turned upon her with newly raised suspicion. Why had she not mentioned the fact before? But something in Mrs. Driver's face deterred him. A woman in these matters sees how the land lies, while the cleverest man is still unable to distinguish it from the clouds upon the horizon-line.

"We are pleased to know you, Harold," said Mrs. Driver, a gentle, soft-voiced motherly person.

"You have really come to practise here?" went on the father, still rather on his guard.

"I wanted sea-air. The change will do me good," replied Harold, rather evasively. "I like the place, too."

Not a doubt of it. Harbridge was after his own heart, and so were some people who lived in it. He found it so much to his taste that he declared within a week or two that he thought of remaining there altogether. He would go into partnership with the local doctor; perhaps he had another partnership also in his eye.

"Can't you see what's going on under your nose, father?" asked Mrs. Driver.

"What do I care? I shall not interfere."

"Mrs. Purling will never give her consent. Poor Doll!"

"*That* for Mrs. Purling and her consent!" said Mr. Driver, snapping his fingers. "Doll is ever so much too good for them — well, not for him; he is an honest, straightforward fellow: but as for that selfish, silly, purse-proud old woman, she may thank Heaven if she gains a daughter like Doll."

That this was not Mrs. Purling's view of the question was plainly evident from a letter which awoke Harold rather rudely from his rosy dreams.

"So at length I have found you out, Harold. I never dreamt you could be so deceitful and double-faced. To talk of clinical lectures in town, and all the time at Harbridge, philandering with that forward, intriguing girl! Only with the greatest difficulty have I succeeded in learning the truth. Phillipa — who, it seems, has known your secret all along, and to whom, I find, you have constantly written — could not continue indifferent to my distress of mind. Although she has shielded you so far with a magnanimity that is truly heroic, she has interposed at length only to save my life.

"I desire you will come to me at once. Do not disobey me, Harold. I am very seriously displeased, and will only consent to forgive the past when I find you ready to bend your stubborn heart to obey my will."

Harold started at once for home. He hoped rather against hope that he might talk his mother over; but her aspect was not encouraging when he met her face to face.

No tragedy-queen could have assumed more scorn. Mrs. Purling, having thrown herself into several attitudes, fell at length into a chair.

"I never thought it," she said; "not from my own and only child. The serpent's tooth hath not such fangs, such power to sting, as the base ingratitude of one undutiful boy. But this fills the cup. I have done with you — for ever, unless you give me your sacred word of honour now, at this minute, never to speak to Dolly Driver again."

"Such a promise would be quite impossible under any circumstances, but I distinctly refuse to give it — upon compulsion."

"Then you have fair warning. Not one penny of my money shall you ever possess. I will never see you again."

"I sincerely trust the last is only an empty threat, my dearest mother."

She made a gesture as though she were not to be beguiled by soft words.

"As for the money, it matters little. Thank God, I have my profession."

"At which you will starve."

"By which I shall earn my bread as my father did. Besides, I can fall back upon the reputation of the Family Pills."

"I see you wish to goad me beyond endurance, Harold. Go!"

"For good and all?"

"Yes; except on the one alternative. Will you give up this idiotic passion? You refuse. It is on your own head, then. Go — go till I send for you, which will be never!"

Harold went without another word — to Harbridge, overcame Dolly's scruples, secured the practice, and within a month was married and settled.

Mrs. Purling, in Phillipa's presence, made a great parade of burning her will.

"He has brought it all on himself, unnatural boy! But you, darling Phillipa, will never treat me thus. *Noblesse oblige.* The bright blue blood that fills your veins would curdle at a *mésalliance*, I know."

Mrs. Purling was quite calm and self-possessed, while Miss Fanshawe, strange to say, seemed agitated enough for both. Her hands trembled, she looked away; only with positive repugnance she submitted to her new mother's affectionate embrace. A woman who is capable of the most cold-blooded calculating intrigue may yet have an access of remorse. Phillipa's heart was heavy now at the moment of her triumph. It cost her more than a passing pang to remember that she had robbed Harold Purling of his birthright, and had turned to her own base purpose the foolish cravings of the silly mother's heart.

But she had put aside self-upbraiding when she met her lover in town.

"Faith, you are a trump, Phillipa; but it's not much too soon. When will you take your reward?"

"Meaning Mr. Jillingham? Is the reward worth taking, I wonder?" For a moment she held him at bay. "Suppose I were to refuse you now at the eleventh hour? It is for you to sue. I am not what I was. Mrs. Purling calls me the heiress of the Purlings, and we may not consider Mr. Gilbert Jillingham a very eligible *parti*."

"You dare not refuse me, Phillipa," said Gilly very seriously. "I should expose your schemes, and we should go to the wall together. No, there is no escape for you now; our interests are identical."

"How am I to introduce you upon the scene?"

"Quite naturally; I shall go and stay at Compton Revel. They will have me, for your sake, if not for my own. I shall begin *de novo* — at the very beginning: be smitten, pay you court, win over the heiress, and propose."

So it fell out, and they also were married before the end of the year.

CHAPTER VI.

Mean as had been their conduct towards Mrs. Purling and her son, Phillipa and her husband were not to be classed with common adventurers of the ordinary type. Born in a lower station, Gilly Jillingham might have taken honours as a "prig"; in his own with less luck he might have been an Ishmaelite generally shunned. Phillipa also might have degenerated into a mere soured cackling hanger-on; but they were not pariahs by caste, but Brahmins, and entitled to all due honour so long as they floated on top of the wave. Perhaps if near drowning no finger would have been outstretched to save; but there were plenty to pat them on the back as they disported themselves on the sound dry land. Fairweather friends and needy relatives rallied round their prosperity, of course; but they were also accepted as successful social facts by the whole of that great world which judges for the most part by appearances, being too idle or too much engrossed by folly to apply more accurate or searching tests. In good society those who cared to talk twice of the matter blamed Harold; he was absent; besides, he had gone to the wall, therefore he must be in the wrong. On the other hand, the Jillinghams deserved the triumph that is never denied success. To Gilly prosperous were forgiven the sins of Gilly in social and moral rags. If scandal like an evil gas had been let loose to crystallise upon Phillipa's good name, the black stains could not adhere long to so charming a person, who made the Purling mansion in Berkeley Square one of the best-frequented and most fashionable in town.

There were many reasons why the Jillinghams should find their account in perpetual junketings. Social excitement was as the breath in Gilly's nostrils; notorious for profuse expenditure even when he was penniless, he was now absolutely reckless with money that was plentiful and moreover not his own. Nor was the constant whirl of gaieties without its charm for Phillipa; it deadened conscience, and consoled in some measure for the neglect and indifference she soon encountered at her husband's hands. But the most potent reason was that it fooled Mrs. Purling to the top of her bent. Self satisfaction beamed upon her ample face as she found herself at length in constant intercourse and on a social equality — as she thought — with the potentates and powers and great ones of the earth. Gilly Jillingham in the days of his apogee had been the spoiled favourite of more than one titled dame; his success must have been great, to measure it by the envy and hatred he evoked among his fellow men — even when in the cold shade there were duchesses who fought for him still; and now, when once more in full blossom, all his fair friends were ready to pet him as of old. The form in which their kindness pleased him best — because it was most to his advantage — was in making much of Mrs. Purling. Great people have the knack of putting those whom they patronise on the very best terms with themselves; and Mrs. Purling was so convinced of her success as a leader of fashion that she would have asked for a peerage in her own right, taking for arms three pills proper upon a silver field, if she could have been certain that these honours would not descend to her recreant son.

Whether or not, as time passed, she was absolutely happy, she did not pause to inquire. The devotion of her newly adopted children was so unstinting, and they kept her so continually busy, that she had not time for self reproach. It was a disappointment to her that the Jillinghams had no prospect of a family, and her chagrin would have been increased had she known that already a boy and girl had been born to the rightful heirs at Harbridge. But such news was carefully kept from her; she was rigorously cut off from all communication with her son. There was no safety otherwise against mischance; the strange processes of the old creature's mind were inscrutable; she might in one spasm of an awakened conscience undo all. For the Jillinghams were still absolutely dependent upon her; she could turn them out of house and home whenever she pleased. A small settlement was all the real property Phillipa had secured. Although with right royal generosity Mrs. Purling gave her favourites a liberal allowance, and promised them everything when she was gone, yet was she like a crustacean in the tenacity of her grip upon her own. This close-fistedness was exceedingly distasteful to Mr. Jillingham. He had an appetite for gold not easily appeased, and four or five thousand a year was to him but a mouthful to be swallowed at one gulp.

Openly of course he continued on his best behaviour, but behind the scenes he permitted himself to grumble loudly at the old lady's meanness and miserly ways.

"I cannot understand you, Gilbert. I cannot see what you do with all the money you get," said Phillipa reproachfully one day when they were alone, and Gilly was enlarging upon his favourite theme. "You live at free quarters, you have no expenses and ought to have no debts."

"Have you no debts, pray?"

"None that you are ignorant of."

"Look here, Phillipa; listen to me. I spend what I please, how I please. I shall give no account of it to you, nor to any one else in the world."

"It is not necessary. I had rather not be told. I

do not care to know," said Phillipa, womanlike, forgetting that she had begun by wishing to be informed. She had her own suspicions, but forbore to question further, lest she might be brought face to face with the outrages she feared he put upon her.

"She will take to counting the potatoes next. It's most contemptible. A mean old brute —"

"I shall not listen to you, Gilbert. You owe her everything."

"Do I? I wonder what my tailor would say to that or Reuben Isaac Melchisedec? I've more than one creditor; they are a prolific and, I am sorry to say, a long-lived race."

"I hope Mrs. Purling may live to be a hundred years at least —"

"I don't. I'd rather she was choked by one of those pills you tell me she takes every morning and night."

There was something in his tone which made Phillipa look at him hard. Was it possible that he contemplated any terrible wickedness? The mere apprehension made her blood run cold.

"O Gilly, swear to me that you will not harbour evil thoughts, that you will put aside the devil who is prompting and luring you to some awful crime!"

"Psha, Phillipa, you ought to have gone into the Church. Moderate your transports — here comes one of the footmen."

"A person to see you, sir," said the servant. "He 'aven't got any card, but his business is very particular."

"I can't see him; send him away. If he won't go call the police."

"Says his name, sir, is Shubenacady."

"Take him to the library; I'll come."

Jillingham's face was rather pale, and his lips were set firm when he met his visitor.

"What the mischief do you want?"

"Five thou — ten — what you please. I know of a splendid investment."

"In soap?"

He was the dirtiest creature that ever was seen. He wore a full suit of black, but the coat and trousers were white with age and dust-stains; an open waistcoat, exposing an embroidered shirt which could not have been washed for months; his hat was napless, and had a limp brim; no gloves, and the grimiest of hands. But he was decorated, and wore a ribbon, probably of St. Lucifer.

"In soap, or shavings, or shoddy; what does it matter to you? When can I have the money?"

"Never; not another sixpence."

"Then I shall publish all I know."

"No one will believe you."

"I have proofs."

"Which are forged. I tell you I'm too strong for you: you will find yourself in the wrong box. I am sick of this; and I mean to put an end to your extortion."

"You dare me. You know the consequences."

"The first consequence will be that I shall give you in charge. Be off!"

"You shall have a week to think better of it."

Gilly rang the bell.

"Shall I send for a policeman, or will you go?"

He went, muttering imprecations inter-mixed with threats; but Gilly Jillingham, quite proud of his courage, seemed for the moment callous to both. He little dreamt how soon the latter would be put into effect.

Within a few days of this interview the greatest event of Mrs. Purling's whole social career was due; she was to entertain royalty beneath her own roof. This crowning of the edi-fice of her ambition filled her with solemn awe; the preparations for the coming ball were stu-pendous, her own magnificent costume seemed made up of diamonds and bullion and five-pound notes.

Long before the hour of reception she might have been seen pacing to and fro with stately splendour, contemplating the daïs erected for royalty at one end of the room, and thinking with a glow of satisfaction that the representa-tive of the Purlings had at last come to her own. At this supreme moment she was grateful to dear Phillipa and to Gilbert little less dear.

Then guests began to pour in. Where was

Phillipa? Very late; she might have dressed earlier. A servant was sent to call her, and Phillipa, hurrying down, met Gilly on the upper floor coming out of Mrs. Purling's bedroom.

"What have you been doing there?" she asked.

"Mrs. Purling wanted a fan," said Gilly readily.

She might want one fan, but hardly two; and had Phillipa been less flurried she might have noticed that Mrs. Purling had one already in her hand. But then their Royal Highnesses arrived; the heiress made her curtsey for the first time in her life, was graciously received, and the hour of her apotheosis had actually come. Presently the crowd became so dense that every inch of space was covered; people overflowed on to the landings, and sat four or five deep upon the stairs. Dancing was simply impossible; however, hundreds of couples went through the form. Phillipa, as in duty bound, remained in the thick of the *mêlée*, but Gilly had very early disappeared. He preferred the card-room; his waltzing days were over, he said. He was playing; it was not very good taste, but there were some men who preferred a quiet rubber to looking at princes or the antics of boys and girls, and he wished to oblige his friends.

"Can you give me a moment, Le Grice?" said Lord Camberwell, coming into the card-room. "I have had a most extraordinary letter. It accuses Gilly Jillingham —"

"God bless my soul," cried old Colonel Le Grice, "a letter of the same sort has been sent to me!"

"Have you had any suspicion that he played unfairly?"

"Not the slightest; I know he always holds the most surprising hands, that he plays for very high stakes, that he nearly always wins —"

"Is he winning now?"

Of course. Mr. Jillingham's luck never deserted him. He was trying now perhaps to make at one coup sufficient to silence for a further space his enemy's tongue; the bets upon the odd trick alone amounted to a thousand or more. But he was too late. His hour had come.

Suddenly Lord Camberwell spoke in a loud peremptory voice:

"Stop! Mr. Jillingham is cheating. He does it in the deal. I have watched him now for three rounds."

"And so have I," added Colonel Le Grice.

Gilly sprang to his feet. For a moment he seemed disposed to brazen it out; then he read his sentence in the face of those who had detected and now judged him. There was no appeal: he was doomed. From henceforth he was socially and morally dead, and, without a word, he slunk away from the house.

The buzz of the ballroom soon caught up the ugly scandal, and tossed it wildly from lip to lip.

"Mr. Jillingham caught cheating at cards!" Everyone said, of course, they had suspected it all along; now every one knew it as a fact, except those most nearly concerned. To them it came last. To Phillipa, whose heart it stabbed as with a knife, cut through and through; then to Mrs. Purling, who, a little taken aback by the sudden exodus of her guests, asked innocently what it meant, upon which some one, without knowing who she was, told her the exact truth.

Quite stunned by the terrible shock, dazed, terrified, was the heiress, scarcely capable of comprehending what had occurred. Then with a sad, scared face, motioning Phillipa on one side, who, equally white and grief-stricken, would have helped her, she crept slowly upstairs, feeling that at one blow the whole fabric of her social repute was tumbled in the dust.

The lights were out, the play was over, the house still and silent, when, with loud shrieks, Mrs. Purling's maid rushed to Phillipa's room.

"Mrs. Purling, ma'am! — my mistress, she is dying! Come to her! She is nearly gone!"

In truth, the poor old woman was in the extremest agony; it was quite terrible to see her. She gasped as if for air; her whole frame jerked and twitched with the violence of her convulsions; gradually her body was drawn in a curve, like that of a tensely strung bow.

The spasms abated, then recommenced;

abated, then raged with increased fury. But through it all she was conscious; she had even the power of speech, and cried aloud again and again, with a bitter heart-wrung cry, for "Harold! Harold!" the absent much-wronged son.

"The symptoms are those of tetanus," said the nearest medical practitioner, who had been called in. He seemed fairly puzzled. "Tetanus or — " He did not finish the sentence, because the single word that was on his lips formed a serious charge against a person or persons unknown. "But there is nothing to explain lockjaw; while the abatement of the symptoms points to —" Again he paused.

The muscles of the mouth, which had been the last attacked, gradually resumed their normal condition. The patient appeared altogether more easy, the writhings subsided; presently, as if utterly exhausted, she sank off to sleep.

Harold Purling had come up post-haste from Harbridge; and when the mother opened her eyes they rested upon her son.

A hurried consultation passed in whispers between the two doctors. Phillipa was present; she and the maid had not left Mrs. Purling all night.

"Mother," said Harold, "you are out of all danger. Tell me — do you recollect taking anything likely to make you ill?"

"Only the pills." She pointed to the family medicine — a box of which stood always by her bedside. She had some curious notion that it was her duty to show belief in the Primeval Pills, and she made a practice of swallowing two morning and night.

Harold opened the box; examined the pills; finally put one into his mouth and bit it through. Bitter as gall.

"They have been tampered with," he said. "These contain strychnia. You have had a narrow escape of being poisoned, dearest mother — poisoned by your own pills!"

He half smiled at the conceit.

"There has been foul play, I swear. It shall be sifted to the bottom, and the guilty called to serious account."

But the mystery was never solved. If Phillipa had in her heart misgivings, she kept her suspicions to herself; no one accused her; there seemed explanation for her cowed and trembling manner in Gilly's downfall and disgrace. The man himself never reappeared openly; only now and again he swooped down and robbed Phillipa of all she, possessed — the thrift of her allowance from Mrs. Purling.

As for the heiress, surrounded by the real love and warm hearts of her lineal descendants, she was satisfied to eschew all further acquaintance with people of the Blue Blood.

THE END

www.ingramcontent.com/pod-product-compliance
Lightning Source LLC
Chambersburg PA
CBHW031902170626
46807CB00004B/1848